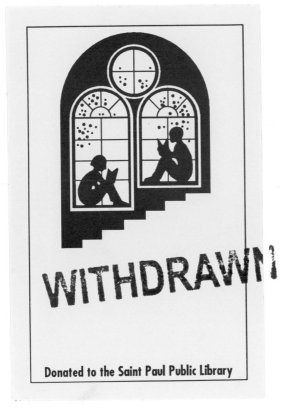

The Bathwater Gang Gets Down to Business

by Jerry Spinelli

Illustrated by Meredith Johnson

Little, Brown and Company

Boston   Toronto   London

First Edition

The characters and events in this book are fictitious.
Any similarity to real persons, living or dead, is
coincidental and not intended by the author.

Library of Congress Cataloging-in-Publication Data

Spinelli, Jerry.
  The Bathwater Gang gets down to business / by Jerry
Spinelli: illustrated by Meredith Johnson. — 1st ed.
    p.   cm.
  Summary: When the Bathwater Gang fails to make money
with its pet-cleaning business, Bertie comes up with a slightly
dishonest idea to ensure success.
  ISBN 0-316-80808-3
  [1. Money-making projects — Fiction.   2. Pets —
Fiction.   3. Gangs — Fiction.]   I. Johnson, Meredith,
ill.   II. Title.
PZ7.S75663Bau   1992
[Fic] — dc20   91-48129

10 9 8 7 6 5 4 3 2 1

WOR

Published simultaneously in Canada
by Little, Brown & Company (Canada) Limited

PRINTED IN THE UNITED STATES OF AMERICA

For Terry and Eileen Persun

1

The alarm clock rang at 6 A.M.

Bertie Kidd leaped out of bed, bolted from her room, and dashed into the bathroom a split second ahead of her father.

"Hey," said Mr. Kidd, "I have to get ready for work."

"So do I!" said Bertie and slammed the door shut.

Once inside the bathroom, Bertie wasn't quite sure what to do. Usually she went from her bed straight down to the kitchen table.

But this day was different. On this bright day in June Bertie would begin her career as a working woman, as president of Bathwater, Inc., pet cleaners.

Bertie knew that grown-ups who went to work always started the day by preparing themselves in the bathroom. As far as Bertie was concerned, being awake was preparation enough. But she wanted to do this right, so she flicked a few drops of water on her face and brushed her teeth and just sort of hung around until her father began pounding on the door.

By the time Bertie came out, her mother was lined up behind her father in the hallway. Both parents scowled after her as she waltzed down the stairs and into the kitchen.

"Granny!" cried Bertie. "What are you doing up so early?"

Granny always slept late. She said it was one of the best benefits of being old.

Granny poured cereal into Bertie's bowl.

"Had to make sure you were ready for your first day on the job. Besides, I'm captain. Got to keep an eye on my troops."

This was true. Granny was captain of the Bathwater Gang.

"But I'm boss of the business, right, Granny?" said Bertie.

"That's right, but that doesn't mean be bossy."

Bertie nodded. "Right. I'll only be bossy if I have to be."

"What's that supposed to mean?"

"I mean, business is business, right, Granny? It's serious stuff. We can't be clowning around. We gotta make money. There's nothing more serious than making money, right, Granny?"

Granny did not answer directly. She gave a small smile. "So, what are you going to do with all your money?"

Bertie gulped cornflakes. "The circus! We're gonna buy six tickets, one for each of us. And the circus is coming Saturday. What's today, Granny?"

"Tuesday."

Bertie counted on her fingers. "Wednesday . . . Thursday . . . Friday. Four days!" She spluttered cornflakes. "Wow! I gotta get going!" She popped up from the table and dashed out the back door. She was halfway down the backyard when she heard her grandmother call. She stopped. "Granny, I'm in a hurry."

Granny sang, "Somebody forgot something."

"What?" Bertie barked. "*What?*"

Granny only smiled. Bertie looked down. What she saw was her Daffy Duck nightshirt and a pair of bare feet. "Oh," she said.

In exactly one hundred and twenty-three seconds Bertie was dashing through the yard again — and again Granny was calling.

Bertie stomped. "Gran-*neee!* What now?"

Granny was holding something in the air.

Bertie came closer. It was a lunch pail, old and black and chipped, with a rounded lid that latched to the bottom. "It was Grandpa's," said Granny. "He wouldn't want you to go to work without it."

Bertie rushed to her grandmother, hugged her, started to dash off again, stopped and turned. "Anything *else?*"

Granny laughed. "Oh, just the balloons. They're in with your lunch."

"Balloons?"

"Sure. For your grand opening. Every grand opening has to have balloons."

Bertie smacked the lunch pail. "Right — thanks!" And off she went.

Bertie ran to the last backyard on the other side of the alley. This would be the location of Bathwater, Inc. It was also the home of Damaris Pickwell, Bertie's best friend.

The Pickwells' white duck, Roscoe, greeted Bertie with a "*Quack.*"

"Quack," said Bertie.

The back door was open. Bertie barged in without knocking. The Pickwells didn't seem to mind people barging into their house.

Bertie ran upstairs and dragged Damaris out of bed. Damaris kept trying to sleep, so Bertie had to dress her. Then Bertie grabbed her under the arms and dragged her down the stairs. By the time they hit bottom, Damaris was awake.

In the backyard Bertie and Damaris lugged out a large, round metal tub. It had been loaned to the gang by Mr. Pickwell, who collected and sold old housewares.

Then Andy Boyer showed up with a scrub brush.

Amy Moss came with a small bottle. She opened the bottle and waved it under the others' noses.

"Smells like an old lady," said Andy.

"Pet perfume," said Amy.

Bertie clapped. "Great! Now we're cookin'!"

Itchy Mills brought flea powder and a stack of old towels and rags.

The final member of the gang, Noodles Overmeyer, brought a supermarket bag.

"Don't tell me that's your lunch," said Bertie.

Noodles merely grinned.

Bertie looked around at her crew, at the beginnings of their business. Suddenly she smacked her forehead. "Oh no!" she wailed. "We forgot the most important thing!"

2

"What's that?" everyone said at once, except Roscoe, who said, "*Quack.*"

"A sign," said Bertie. "Whoever heard of a business without a sign?"

Into the Pickwell house ran the six kids. Out they came with a cardboard box, a pair of scissors, and a felt-tip marker.

Andy Boyer cut one side out of the box. Bertie gave the marker to Amy Moss. "Here. You're the neatest writer."

Bertie told Amy what to write. The sign looked like this:

Bertie nailed the sign to the telephone pole in front of the Pickwells' house. In the backyard Andy Boyer filled the round tub with water from the garden hose. Damaris poured in two cupfuls of bubble bath. Then the whole gang plunged arms in to the elbows and swished around until the tub had a foamy dome two feet high.

Bertie clapped. "All *right* — we're open for business!"

"All *right!*" cheered the gang.

Bertie smacked her forehead. "*Not* all right."

She took off. She ran all the way home. She returned with her old toolbox, from the

10

days when she used to play carpenter.

"What's that?" said Itchy Mills.

"Money box," said Bertie. She plunked it down. "*Now* we're open for business."

"I can see that circus already," said Andy Boyer.

Amy Moss giggled. "I'm already laughing at the clowns. I hope they have monkeys."

"I can taste that cotton candy," said Noodles.

"How much money do we need to buy tickets?" said Damaris.

"Who cares?" said Bertie. "We have four whole days. We'll make so much money we'll be able to buy the *circus!*"

"I could eat a circus," said Noodles. "Is it lunchtime yet?"

Bertie glared at Noodles. The others laughed.

Andy Boyer was the only one with a watch. He kept announcing the time every

fifteen minutes. When he announced, "Ten o'clock," Bertie said, "Something's wrong. The money should be pouring in by now. Amy, go see if the sign is still there."

Amy reported that the sign was still there.

Bertie sighed. She walked off by herself to think. Suddenly she whirled. She smacked her forehead. "Ach! What a dumbo. I forgot."

3

Bertie sent Amy to get the sign, gave her the felt-tip marker, and told her what to do. Soon the sign was back on the pole.

"People love grand openings," said Bertie. She blew up the balloons from her lunch pail and tacked them to the pole. "Let's get ready for the mobs!"

The gang raced to the backyard. They swished up the suds, which had fallen flat.

When Andy announced, "Ten-thirty," Bertie announced, "Coffee break!"

"Yahoo!" yelled Noodles. He tore open his lunch bag.

"I'm not allowed to drink coffee," said Damaris.

"You don't have to," said Bertie. "It's just called that. You have to stop your business at ten-thirty. Grown-ups have coffee. We can just have a snack." She opened her lunch pail. "Okay, everybody, snack time." She glared at Noodles. "And *snack* means *snack*."

Noodles, chewing away, said, "Tuh thuh thuh huffuh thuhnuh."

Bertie winced. "Huh?"

Itchy translated. Itchy was the only person in Two Mills who could understand Noodles Overmeyer with a mouth full of food. "He says three sandwiches is a snack for him."

Bertie rolled her eyes.

The gang ate their snacks and talked about the circus and glanced about for the first signs of a mob.

When a factory whistle blew in the distance, Noodles said, "That means it's twelve o'clock noon. That means lunchtime."

But nobody, not even Noodles, reached for lunch. They all stared at the empty money box.

Just then Captain Granny came wogging by in her bright pink sweatsuit. To Granny, wogging meant faster than walking and slower than jogging. "Hey," she said, pulling to a stop, "why all the glum faces?"

"You'd be glum, too," said Bertie, "if you had a business and nobody came. It's already lunchtime and we don't have a single customer."

"Do you have a sign up?" said Granny.

"Yes."

"Balloons?"

"Yes."

"Well," said Granny, "let's take a look-see."

She led the gang out to the sign. She studied it for a minute. "Aha!" She held out her hand. "Give me a marker."

Amy gave her the marker. Granny added a single word to the sign:

"That'll do the trick," said Granny. "'Only.' It's the magic word. You never give a price without the word 'only.' That makes it sound cheaper."

"Like, *only* a million dollars?" quipped Itchy.

"Exactly," said Granny. "See ya!" And off she went a-wogging.

Bertie clapped her hands. "Okay! Let's finish lunch fast. They're gonna be mobbing us any minute now."

The gang wolfed down their lunches and waited for the mob.

And waited . . .

And waited . . .

4

Itchy cried out: "I can't stand this waiting!" He tore off his sneakers and socks and rolled up his pant legs and jumped into the tub. "I gotta wash something, even if it's my own feet."

This was too much for Noodles. He also whipped off his sneaks and socks and jumped in.

Within moments everyone but Bertie was in the tub. In fact, Andy was doing a handstand.

"Come on, Bert!" they called.

Bertie shook her head. "Not me. I'm the boss. I gotta be diggified."

So Roscoe squeezed into the last remaining space.

Bertie did not remain dignified for long, not after the soapsuds and tub-water fight began. She was right in the middle of it, yelling, "Hey, this is supposed to be business, not fun!"

Itchy grabbed the pet perfume, and soon everyone, including Roscoe, smelled like lilies.

"Hey," said Andy, "why don't we practice washing stuff so we'll be ready when the real pets show up?"

Everyone agreed. In time a row of teddy bears and dinosaurs was dripping and drying on the clothesline. Plus one long red wig — Granny's — which she used to wear quite often but now saved for special occasions.

Andy still wasn't satisfied. "We gotta practice on something live." Others looked at

Roscoe, but Andy looked at Bertie. "Wilma!"

"Oh no," said Bertie. "Forget Wilma."

Wilma was Bertie's pet worm.

Andy argued his case. Wilma, he pointed out, had been living in dirt all her life. Surely by now she could use a bath.

Bertie had to admit that Andy's argument made sense. She ran home to fetch Wilma. When she returned, she had a Polaroid camera as well.

Bertie took a picture of Wilma. Then she dipped wormy, wiggling Wilma in the suds, rinsed her off, and took another picture.

"Before and after," Bertie explained. "This will show everybody what a good job we do."

Bertie tacked the before and after pictures of Wilma to the sign out front.

The factory whistle blew its flute-like note over Two Mills.

Bertie groaned. "Oh no. Five o'clock." She gazed forlornly at the money box. "We didn't make a measly cent."

"And now only three days till the circus," grumped Damaris.

While the others cleaned up, Bertie walked out front. She looked at the sign. Throughout the afternoon Bertie had come out and reduced the price. At Granny's suggestion she had even added a second sign, with just one word, which Granny called "every shopper's magic word":

Nothing had worked. Even the balloons had lost their puff and hung limp and defeated.

All over town, workers were heading happily home, the factory whistle music to their ears. To Bertie, it was only a sad, sad song.

And then, as her eyes swung toward Elm Street, she saw a familiar vehicle go by. It was the ice-cream truck.

Bertie got an idea.

5

When the Bathwater Gang reported for work at Damaris Pickwell's backyard next morning, they found Bertie waiting with the biggest wagon they had ever seen.

"What's that for?" asked Andy.

"If the customers won't come to us," said Bertie, "we'll just have to go to the customers."

She told them how she and Granny had worked until ten o'clock the night before, widening the wagon with a platform of wood and building up the sides. "So, let's get going," she said, clapping her hands. "Load 'er up!"

The gang put the tub and pet-washing equipment aboard. The tub, empty after the previous day's water fight, had to be refilled and re-foamed.

When all was ready, Bertie flung her arm out and called: "Onward!"

The gang was on the move. A new sign rode like a sail above the wagon's back panel.

Going Out of
BUSINESS
Sale
Wash Your pet
ONLY $1

"Hey," said Andy, "we're not going out of business."

"I know that," said Bertie. "But Granny says going-out-of-business sales are the best sales of all."

The washer wagon rolled out Chain Street

to Elm, then up the long Elm Street hill.

"Okay," said Bertie, "let's let 'em know we're here." She pulled a kazoo from her lunch pail. "I'll toot. Everybody else call it out, like the hot-dog guy at the ball park."

Bertie tooted on the kazoo, and the gang called it out:

"Hey — hey — get yer pets washed right here! Right here!"

"Big sale! Goin' outta business! Step right up!"

"Only a dollar! One tiny, measly, silly old dollar!"

Up Elm . . . over Buttonwood . . . down Oak . . . over Oriole . . . up Marshall. They saw some pets, but none that appeared to need a bath. Not a single customer came forth.

As they were passing Marshall Manor, a voice called to them: "Yoo-hoo." It came from a white-haired woman sitting in a wheelchair on the porch.

Bertie climbed the porch steps. "Do you have a pet?" she said.

"Oh yes," said the white-haired lady. "I have an adorable pet."

"Well, we wash pets. Would you like us to wash yours?"

"Oh yes! That would be wonderful."

Bertie looked around. She did not see any animals. "Would you like to give your pet to us? We'll get started."

"Oh yes indeed," said the lady. She reached into the handbag on her lap and pulled out her pet.

Bertie boggled. "Is that" — she gulped — "a *m-mouse?*"

For a moment the lady seemed puzzled. "A mouse? Oh — a *mouse.* Well, I suppose so. But I don't think of her that way. I just think of her as Elizabeth." She held out the mouse.

Bertie knew she could not back out now. She forced her lips to smile and closed her eyes as the wriggling, surprisingly furry little

creature was placed in her hands.

She turned. She descended the steps slowly, stiffly, holding the snow-white, pink-eyed squirmer at arm's length, as though the slightest jolt might make it explode.

As she neared the wagon, her horror-struck business partners all took a giant step backward.

"Oh no," whispered Itchy.

"Not me," whispered Noodles and Amy.

Bertie gave them her fiercest glare. Andy was the first to cave in. He came forward. He took a deep breath. "You dunk it." He took a towel from the wagon. "I'll dry."

Bertie nodded. She raised the mouse over the tub. "Ready?"

Andy croaked, "Ready."

It was over in five seconds. A quick dunk into the sudsy water, and a gentle mauling with the towel.

Bertie returned the mouse to the lady, who squealed with delight and returned Elizabeth to her handbag. She pulled out five pennies and gave them to Bertie with a big smile. "Is that too much?"

Bertie stared at the pennies. "Oh no," she said. She backed down the steps. "Mice are five cents apiece."

The gang waved and moved on up Marshall. Bertie deposited the pennies in the money box. "At this rate," she grumbled, "we'll make it to *next* year's circus."

She grabbed a marker, turned the sign around, and wrote a new one:

"From now on," said Bertie, "you're gonna have to be a caterpillar to get off that cheap."

The gang rolled on.

Two blocks later, their luck changed.

6

"You think it's real?" asked Itchy.

"Maybe we're seeing things because we're hungry," said Noodles.

What appeared to them was a dog, standing on the corner of Marshall and Noble, staring at them. And not just any dog. A dirty dog.

"Maybe it's a mirage," said Damaris.

Bertie yelled, "Let's find out!"

The gang took off. The dog took off.

"It's real!" yipped Itchy.

The dog ran out Noble, down Elm, over

Oriole, back to Elm. Noodles was pulling the wagon, so he lagged behind the others.

Often the dog would wait for them to catch up. Then it would bolt as the bath wagon drew near.

Suddenly Bertie slammed on her brakes. "Hold it!" She smacked her forehead. "What dumbos! Why are *we* chasing *him?* Who brought candy for lunch?"

"Milky Way," said Itchy.

"Get it," said Bertie.

Reluctantly, Itchy got the candy bar from his lunch bag in the wagon. He gave it to Bertie. Bertie unwrapped it and held it out. "Come on, doggie, come on."

The dog trotted right up to Bertie. Within seconds, it was in the tub, munching Milky Way while the gang scrubbed.

As the kids were drying off a clean brown-and-white dog, a red-haired boy came running. "Hey! What are you doing with my dog?"

"We just washed him," Bertie said pleasantly. She pointed to the sign on the wagon. "That's us. He's clean as a whistle now." She spread her hands to span the dog from tail to nose. "How long is he? About thirty inches? How much is five cents times thirty inches . . . anybody?"

The boy glared at her. "Who asked you to wash my dog?"

Bertie moved her hands closer. "You know, come to think of it, he really only looks about twenty inches long."

"Maybe I *want* him dirty."

"Okay, ten inches. That's as cheap —" The rest of the sentence stuck in her throat, for the boy was picking up a handful of dirt and pouring it over his pet. He sneered, "I'll wash my own dog."

The boy and his dog were a block away by the time the gang came out of their daze.

Andy rattled the money box. "Five measly pennies."

"Good-bye, circus," sighed Damaris.

"Good-bye, cotton candy," sighed Noodles.

"Wrong," said Bertie. "Hel-*lo*, circus."

The others stared at her, but she was staring at the ground.

7

Next day — Thursday — the gang was out again, but the wagon was different. Gone were the tub and wash tools and sign. In their place was a bed of mud, a mattress of muck.

"It's not right," said Damaris. "It's cheating."

"It's business," said Bertie.

The two best friends had been arguing since the night before.

"It's not honest," said Damaris.

"Honest has nothing to do with it," said Bertie. "Business is business. Everything counts."

"We could go to jail," said Damaris.

Bertie slapped her forehead. "Aye yi yi! I don't believe this. Listen" — she poked Damaris in the chest — "you want to go to the circus, don't you?"

Damaris blinked. "Yes." She slapped Bertie's finger away. "But who made you the boss?"

Bertie screeched. "Who? *I* made me the boss."

"I thought Granny was the boss."

Bertie sighed. "Read my lips. Granny is captain of the gang. I am boss of the business."

"Well, I don't like bosses."

"Well, tough cookies. You can't have a business without a boss. Do you want to quit?"

Damaris's lip quivered. "I didn't say that."

Bertie tested the mud with her fingertip. "Well, we gotta get moving. Everybody that wants to work, follow me."

Bertie pulled the wagon along. Everyone went with her but Damaris.

Then, after a minute, she ran to catch up.

The gang stuck to the alleyways, the backyards: prime pet territory. The first one they came to was Jerry Beeber's little white toy terrier, Sparkles, yipping and licking their fingers through the back fence. Bertie opened the gate, bowed, swept her arm toward the wagon and said, "After you, Sparkles."

Sparkles hopped into the wagon, where he had a marvelous time frolicking in the mud. When Bertie led him back to his yard, Sparkles was no longer sparkling.

Meanwhile, on the street side of the Beeber house, Andy was slipping a flyer into the mailbox:

Pet dirty?
We will clean it.
813 Chain St.

In that block alone the gang found three more pets: two dogs and a box turtle.

Bertie squealed, "We're cookin'!"

Down the alleys they traveled, bringing joy to every animal that loved mud, and to some that didn't. Sometimes they came to a house where they knew a pet lived, but the pet was inside. In such cases, Bertie would ring the doorbell, hand the resident a flyer, and talk some business. Meanwhile, the others were slipping in the back door, snatching the pet, mudding it, and returning it.

Once, they even did it with a hermit crab, dipping it into the mud like a strawberry into chocolate.

When the noontime whistle blew, Bertie called, "About face! Let's get back. We're in business!"

She was right. Four customers were already waiting in the Pickwells' backyard.

All afternoon they kept coming: muddy dogs, cats, turtles, rabbits, hamsters, guinea pigs, gerbils, three mice, two snakes, a hermit crab, a skunk, and a parakeet.

Noodles measured each pet with a ruler. Itchy figured out the price.

Andy kept wishing for a python, but the only two snakes that showed up were garter snakes at forty cents apiece.

At dinner-whistle time, Bertie gathered the gang around the money box. They counted the money in a chorus:

". . . twenty-nine . . . thirty . . . thirty-one . . . thirty-two dollars and ten . . . fifteen . . . twenty cents!"

"We're rich!" exclaimed Itchy.

"Circus, here we come!" cheered Noodles.

Damaris was quiet but beaming.

"And we'll make twice as much," squealed Bertie, "because we'll do it again tomorrow."

"Oh no, you won't," said a grown-up voice.

8

The kids looked up from the pile of money. It was Granny. She was not happy.

"You're giving back every penny," she told them. "You're not running a business, you're running a flimflam. You're cheating your own neighbors, just to make some money. I used to be proud to be your captain, but I'm not proud anymore. "In fact, I'm thinking about resigning." She turned and walked away.

"See *that*, Bertie Kidd!" wailed Damaris. "You and your *'business* is *business.'* You had to be *boss. Now* look what happened!"

Bitter tears stung Bertie's eyes. She could

not speak.

In grim silence the Bathwater Gang gathered up the money and headed for the streets. It was nearly dark before all the ill-gotten money had been returned. The five pennies from washing Elizabeth the mouse once again rattled hollowly in the money box.

Later that night Granny came to sit on the side of Bertie's bed. "It's not the end of the world," she said. "You can still go to the circus with the rest of the family."

Bertie snuffled into her pillow. "I'm staying home. I'm a cheat and I'm greedy and I made you resign. I'm punishing myself by not going to the circus."

"Well," said Granny gently, "since you gave the money back, I've decided to stay on as captain."

Bertie would not be comforted. "A person like me shouldn't be allowed to do anything. I'm never getting out of bed for the rest of my life." She pounded the pillow. "I stink."

For a while Granny said nothing. Then she smiled and bent over and kissed her granddaughter. "Good-night, stinky." She turned off the light and went out.

Bertie did not get out of bed the next morning. Granny brought her breakfast on a tray.

"I don't deserve breakfast," grumbled Bertie.

"Oh?" said Granny. "Well, I do." Granny ate the breakfast.

Later, when Granny brought up a lunch tray, she said, "Do you deserve lunch?"

"No."

So she ate that, too.

"The parade is starting soon," said Granny. "Are you coming with me?"

"No."

When the circus came to town each summer, it paraded up Main Street. The townspeople were invited to march along.

Ten minutes later Granny called up from outside Bertie's bedroom window: "Here I

go! Good-bye!"

By the time Granny had gone two blocks, Bertie was alongside her.

Main Street was already mobbed. Leading the parade was an elephant with a saddle sign saying "Dolly." Behind Dolly walked a baby elephant named Dilly. Dilly held on to Dolly's tail with her trunk.

Then came the rest of the circus troupe: five ponies, a dozen dancing dogs, a llama, a monkey, and a camel, not to mention clowns and acrobats in glittering satins. And the kids of Two Mills — on bikes, on skateboards, on foot, many with their own animals.

Granny stepped into the street. "Come on."

Bertie shook her head. "I'm just watching."

"Party pooper," said Granny.

Bertie watched her grandmother march up the middle of Main Street, waving at the crowd.

9

The parade was gone. The people were gone. Bertie sat on the curb, her elbows on her knees, her chin cupped in her hands.

Where had she gone wrong? All she had wanted to do was make a little money so the gang could go to the circus. Instead, she had let the gang down. They probably hated her. She didn't blame them.

She dragged herself up from the curb. A breeze coming down Main Street brought her a whiff of elephant. Bertie felt like crying, but instead she stomped her foot and shouted for all the world to hear: "Phooey!"

She wandered off. She did not especially notice where she was going, and she didn't care. She figured she would just keep walking, maybe all the way to the ocean, then into the ocean, never to be seen again. The headlines would say:

GREEDY GIRL DROWNS
GOOD RIDDANCE!

Or maybe she would get kidnapped by aliens, hauled off to another planet, and turned into a three-headed mushroom or something.

A crushed soda can lay on the sidewalk. "Litterbug," whispered Bertie. She was about to pick it up when she got a better idea. She kicked it. She would kick it all the way to the ocean or the North Pole, whichever came first.

50

She kicked the crushed can down one sidewalk and up the next, across the streets and over the curbs. One time she wound up and gave it her biggest kick. The can skittered past seven or eight houses before coming to rest — at the foot of the red-haired boy whose dog they had chased.

The boy looked at the can. He looked at Bertie. He nudged the can forward till he was about ten feet from her. Then he kicked it to her.

Bertie did not know what to do. She just stood there for a minute. Then she did two things: she said, "I don't like you," and she kicked the can back at him.

"I'm heartbroken," said the boy. He kicked the can back.

"It's all your fault," said Bertie.

"That so?"

"Yeah. You put dirt on your dog and that gave me an idea and we made all kinds of money and then we had to give it all back and now I'm in big trouble." She kicked the can, hard.

The boy shrugged. "If you minded your own business, you wouldn't be in trouble."

"I *was* minding my business. My business is dirty dogs."

"Not *my* dirty dog."

They kicked the can back and forth for a while without speaking.

"Going to the circus?" he said.

"No. You?"

"Yeah. I'm going to be an elephant trainer. I love elephants."

"I'm gonna be a three-headed mushroom."

More kicks, no talking.

"My name's Robert," he said.

"My name's Alberta." She kicked and wondered, Now, why did I say that? I never call myself that. "Can you touch your nose with your tongue?" she said.

"No."

"Didn't think so. I can." She showed him.

Kicks, clattering can.

"Well, anyway," she said, "I still don't like you."

"I don't like you either."

Bertie stared at the crushed can. The five o'clock factory whistle blew. She picked up the can and ran home.

Granny was even later than Bertie for dinner. After dinner Granny led her to the living room. Her face was serious. "Are you a good enough boss to follow instructions?"

Bertie wasn't sure how to answer. At last she gave a small nod.

"Okay. Here's what you do. You call the gang members right now. Tell them to meet you at the circus tomorrow morning at seven o'clock sharp. Ask for Mr. Howard."

Bertie stared. "What's this all about?"

"Seven sharp," said Granny.

10

The Bathwater Gang arrived at the circus at 7 A.M. sharp. The tents, the circus hands, the animals, were all up.

They found Mr. Howard and introduced themselves. Directing himself to Bertie, Mr. Howard said, "I understand that you're in the pet-washing business."

Bertie glanced at her friends. "Yes, *sir*."

"Okay, here's the deal. You do the job, and each of you gets a free ticket to the big top plus five dollars' worth of refreshments. Interested?"

Bertie clapped. "It's a deal!" She thrust out her hand. Mr. Howard shook it.

"This way," said Mr. Howard. He led them through a maze of trailers and trucks and the smells of animals and frying bacon. "Here's the pet," he said as they rounded a corner.

The gang gaped. The pet was Dilly, the pint-sized elephant.

"These boys'll show you what to do," said Mr. Howard, and he was gone.

The "boys" Mr. Howard referred to were animal handlers washing Dolly nearby. Two of them came over with scrub brushes, pails of soapy water, and a hose.

The gang just stood there, still gaping, until Dilly swung her trunk around, lifted Itchy's shirt, and tickled him on the stomach. Itchy howled with laughter, and the gang set to work.

Six kids giving one elephant a bath — it was a sight. Dilly might have been little for an elephant, but she was big for an animal, much taller than any of the kids, so there was a lot to wash.

They rubbed and they scrubbed until Dilly was brimming with bubbles.

A handler held out the hose. "Okay, who wants to rinse?"

Six kids shouted, "I do!"

As the handler wondered what to do, Bertie suddenly pointed to him and said sternly, "Hold that hose. Don't let anybody touch it."

All eyes followed Bertie as she walked over to a red-haired boy standing nearby.

"Hi, Robert," she said.

"Hi, Alberta," he said.

"You can call me Bertie."

"You can call me Robert."

They laughed.

"I have an idea," said Bertie.

"You're going to throw dirt on the elephant."

Bertie laughed. "No, you dumbo."

"So what is it?"

"*We* washed your *dog,* right?"

"Right."

"So now" — Bertie took Robert by the hand and led him over to the group — "*you* wash our *elephant.*" She put the hose in Robert's hand.

Dilly swung her head toward Robert. Robert's eyes were wonderstruck.

"If you're gonna train 'em," said Bertie, "you gotta wash 'em first."

With a grin as big an an elephant's ear, Robert aimed the hose at Dilly and sent a stream of water onto her rump. Dilly hoisted her trunk and let out a bugle blast of delight.

When their work was done, the gang met with Mr. Howard. Mr. Howard counted them. "Weren't there six before?"

"One of us came late," Bertie told him. "Now there's seven."

Mr. Howard looked a little doubtful. But

he counted out seven tickets and handed them over, plus five dollars' worth of refreshment tickets for each.

"This makes you a member of the gang," Bertie told Robert.

"But I can't," said Robert. "I'm just visiting. I go home in two weeks."

"No sweat," said Bertie. She turned to the others. "Everybody in favor of having a two-week member, raise your hand."

All hands shot up.

"Yahoo!" piped Noodles. "Let's eat!"

That afternoon the Bathwater Gang laughed and cheered and clapped under the big top. They cheered loudest of all when the elephants came on. When Dilly passed by, they all stood and called her name. They were sure she waved back at them.

Other Springboard Books® You Will Enjoy, Now Available in Paperback: